LEGO®

JURASSIC WORLD

BUILD YOUR OWN ADVENTURE

CONTENTS

D1533773

MEET OWEN GRADY

I NEVER HAVE A DULL DAY!

Owen Grady is a dinosaur trainer and researcher at Jurassic World. He is an expert in dinosaur behavior and knows just how to handle them. Owen is brave and confident and is often asked to help if there is a dinosaur emergency in the park.

Wavy hair

Just the right amount of stubble

Vest with pockets for dinosaur treats

Tough, practical jeans

OWEN'S COMPANIONS

Owen's special project is to train four newly hatched baby Raptors. The most intelligent baby Raptor is Blue, who Owen takes with him on his adventures. Owen loves animals and also has a trusty pet dog named Red.

MEET THE TEAM

Although the dinosaurs are the main stars of Jurassic World, a dedicated team works behind the scenes to make a visit to the park truly unforgettable. Look out for these characters as you journey through the LEGO® Jurassic World™ adventure!

RUURK!

CLAIRE DEARING

Claire is the Assistant Manager of Park Operations at Jurassic World. It is her job to make sure things run smoothly in the park. Claire is smart, courageous, and stong-minded. When she and Owen work as a team, nothing can stop them!

VIC HOSKINS

As Head of Security, Vic's job is to make sure that the dinosaur paddocks are secure—so that the tourists will keep coming! A bit of a bully, he thinks he can control the dinosaurs, but he is actually scared of them and has a lot to learn!

DR. WU

Dr. Wu is the Lead Scientist at the Hammond Creation Lab. He is in charge of the project that brings dinosaurs back to life by using prehistoric DNA. The lab's dinosaur creations are getting larger and fiercer!

SIMON MASRANI

As the owner of Jurassic World, Simon wants the park to be a success and is eager to attract new visitors. He encourages the creation of ever-fiercer dinosaurs and impressive new attractions, such as the new playground area.

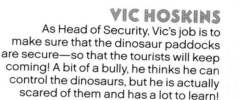

DANNY NEDERMEYER

Danny is the IT technician. His job is to look after the computers and paddock-locking systems—and to do many other odd jobs! Danny secretly dislikes Jurassic World and tries to cause trouble in the park whenever he can.

I JUST GOT AN AMAZING IDEA!

BUILD YOUR OWN ADVENTURE

In the pages of this book, you will discover an exciting LEGO® Jurassic World™ adventure. You will also see some clever ideas for models that might inspire you to create your own. Building LEGO models from your imagination is endlessly fun. There are no limits to what you can build. This is your adventure, so jump right in and start building!

THIS GIVES ME AN IDEA!

HOW TO USE THIS BOOK

This book will not show you exactly how to build the models, because you may not have the same bricks in your LEGO collection. It will give you lots of ideas and show you some useful building tips and model breakdowns that will help you when it comes to building your own models. Here's how the pages work.

Sometimes, different views of the same model are shown

Special features or elements on models are annotated

Breakdowns of models feature useful build tips

"What will you build?" flashes give you even more ideas for models you could make

WHAT WILL YOU BUILD?

MEET THE BUILDER

Rod Gillies is a LEGO fan and super-builder, and he made the inspirational LEGO models that can be found in this book. To make the models just right for this book, Rod worked with the LEGO Jurassic World team at the LEGO Group headquarters in Billund, Denmark. Use Rod's creations to inspire your own models!

BEFORE YOU BEGIN

Here are five handy hints to keep in mind every time you get out your bricks and prepare to build:

LEGO BRICKS ARE THE DNA OF ... LEGO BUILDS!

Organize your bricks
Organizing bricks into colors and types can save you time when you're building.

Make your model stable
Make a model that's sturdy enough to play with. You'll find useful tips in this book for making a stable model.

Be creative
If you don't have the perfect piece, find a creative solution! Look for a different piece that can create a similar effect.

Research
Look up pictures of what you want to build online or in books to inspire your ideas.

Have fun
Don't worry if your model goes wrong. Turn it into something else or start again. The fun is in the building!

TILE

When you want a smooth finish to your build, you need to use a tile. Printed tiles add extra detail to your models.

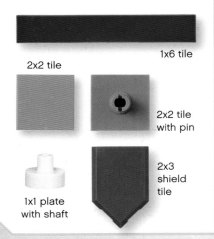

1x6 tile

2x2 tile

2x2 tile with pin

1x1 plate with shaft

2x3 shield tile

BUILDER TALK

Did you know that LEGO® builders have their own language? You will find the terms below used a lot in this book. Here's what they mean.

STUD

Round raised bumps on top of bricks and plates are called studs. A chain has a single stud at each end. Studs fit into "tubes," which are on the bottom of bricks and plates.

Chain

Small leaf piece

2x2 corner plate

1x1 round plate

MEASUREMENTS

Builders describe the size of LEGO® pieces according to the number of studs on them. If a brick has 2 studs across and 3 up, it's a 2x3 brick. If a piece is tall, it has a third number that is its height in standard bricks.

2x3 brick

1x1x5 brick

CLIP

Some pieces have clips on them. You can fit other elements into these clips. Pieces such as ladders fasten onto bars using built-in clips.

1x1 plate with clip

1x1 plate with clip

2x3 tile with clips

HOLE

Bricks and plates with holes are very useful. They will hold bars or LEGO® Technic pins or connectors.

1x1 brick with hole

2x3 curved plate with hole

2x2 round grooved brick with cross axle hole

4x4 round brick with cross axle hole

Ladder with two clips

SIDEWAYS BUILDING

Sometimes you need to build in two directions. That's when you need bricks or plates like these, with studs on more than one side.

1x4 brick with side studs

1x1 brick with two side studs

1x2/2x2 angle plate

1x1 brick with one side stud

Small parts and small balls can cause choking if swallowed. Not for children under 3 years.

BRICK

Where would a builder be without the brick? It's the basis of most models and it comes in a huge variety of shapes and sizes.

 1x1 headlight brick

 2x2 domed brick

2x2 brick

 1x2 textured brick

1x2 grooved brick

1x1 round brick

PLATE

Like bricks, plates have studs on top and tubes on the bottom. A plate is thinner than a brick— the height of three plates is equal to one standard brick.

3 plates = 1 brick

 1x2 jumper plate

 2x3 plate

 2x4 angled plate

 1x1 tooth plate

 2x2 round plate

 1x8 plate with side rail

 1x1 round plate

 1x2 plate with top ring

 4x4 curved plate

 4x4 round plate

SPECIAL PIECES

These special pieces are perfect to use in your own LEGO Jurassic World creations.

 2x2 printed tile

 Plant grass stem

 Minifigure drill

 Egg piece

 White short bone piece

BAR

Bars are useful for building long, thin features but are also used with clips to create angles and moving parts. Bars are the perfect size to fit minifigure hands.

 Bar

 Bar with side studs

 1x2 plate with bar

 1x2 plate with handle

SLOPE

Slopes are bigger at the bottom than on top. Inverted slopes are the same but upside down. They are smaller at the bottom and bigger on top.

 1x2 slope

1x2 inverted slope

HINGE

If you want to make a roof that opens or give a creature a tail that moves, you need a hinge. A ball joint does the same job, too.

 1x2 hinge brick and 1x2 hinge plate

 Hinge plates

 Ball joint socket

 1x2 tow plate with ball joint

 1x2 hinge brick and 2x2 hinge plate

 Hinge cylinder

 1x2 plate with click hinge

CHAPTER 1
A GENTLE GIANT MYSTERY

JURASSIC WORLD

Welcome to Jurassic World! Located on Isla Nublar, this is the only theme park in the world where visitors can get up close to mighty dinosaurs. Today is a special day—it's the grand opening of a new playground area, and the park is packed with tourists. Owen, the expert dinosaur trainer, is going to be busy!

DINOSAURS ARE AWESOME!

OWEN'S OFF-ROADER

Owen relies on his all-terrain 4x4 to get around Isla Nublar. It has big wheels to grip rough ground and bars on the front for pushing through thick vegetation.

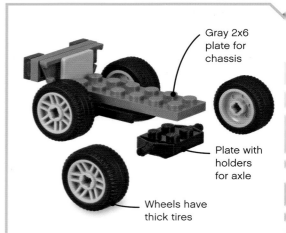

Gray 2x6 plate for chassis

Plate with holders for axle

Wheels have thick tires

4X4 AXLES AND WHEELS

Get the Jurassic World off-roader moving by attaching simple axles to the vehicle's chassis and then pushing wheels onto the axles.

ISLAND VEGETATION

The planners of Jurassic World worked hard to create a lush rain forest habitat where their dinosaurs can feel at home. Build some leafy, spiky, and curly plants in all shades of green.

Large green bush

Spiky sword leaf with clip

Round red plate looks like siren light

FOUR WHEELS OF AWESOMENESS!

Transparent panel for windshield

Two green plates form base

Plate with handle supports leaf

Black bumper

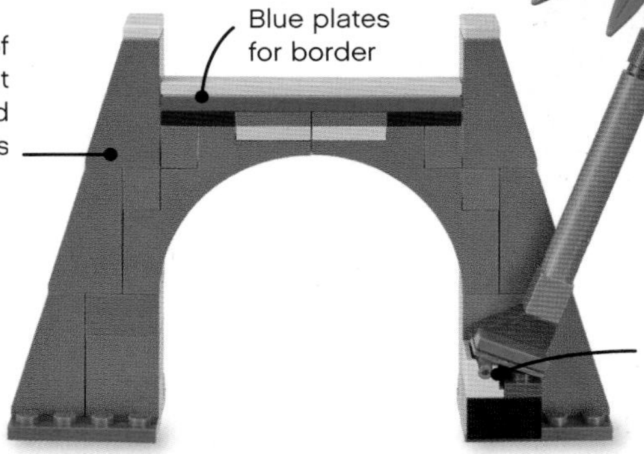

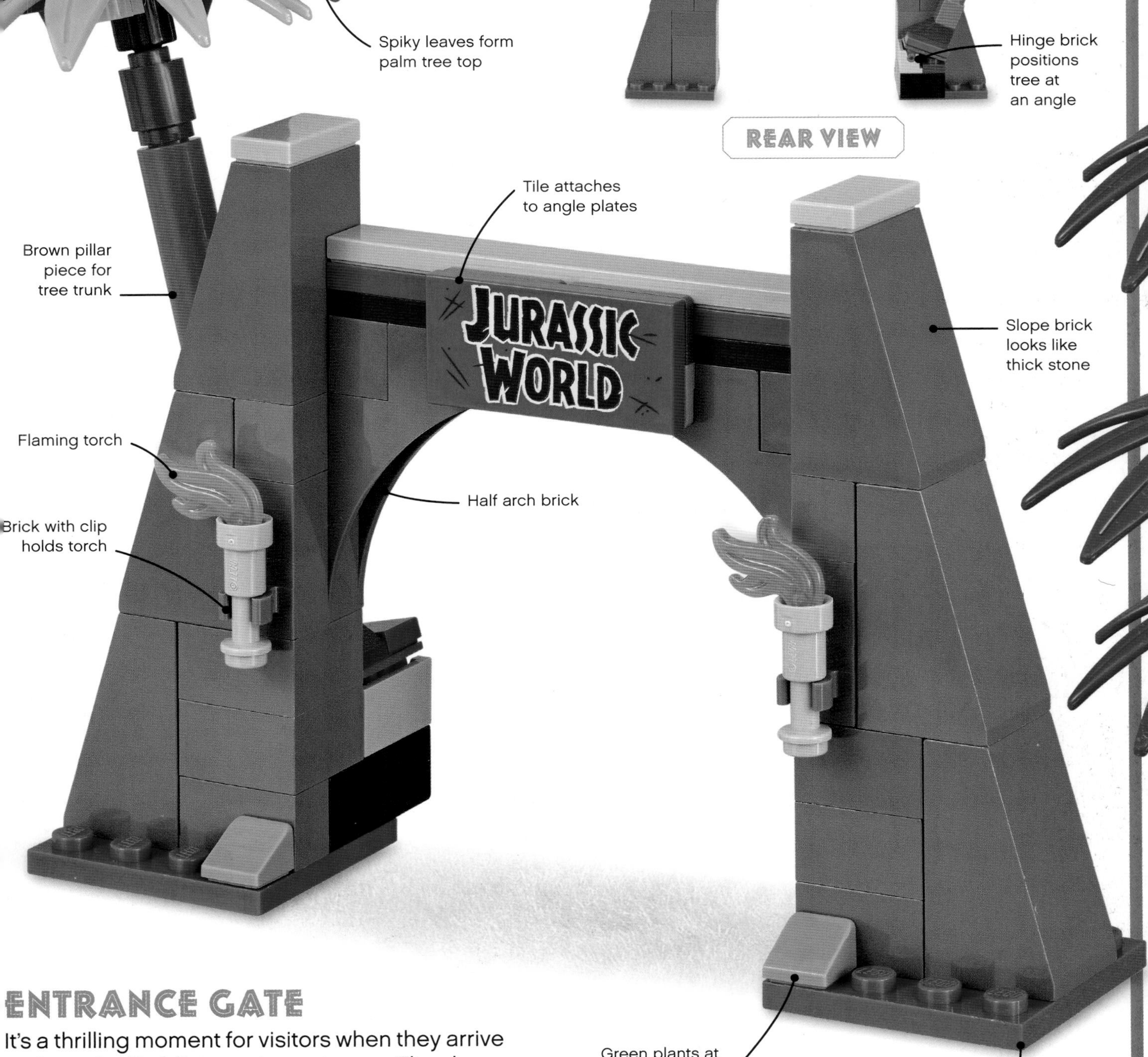

Bricks of different sizes and shapes

Blue plates for border

REAR VIEW

Hinge brick positions tree at an angle

Spiky leaves form palm tree top

Tile attaches to angle plates

Brown pillar piece for tree trunk

Slope brick looks like thick stone

JURASSIC WORLD

Flaming torch

Half arch brick

Brick with clip holds torch

Green plants at ground level

4x4 plate is gate's sturdy base

ENTRANCE GATE

It's a thrilling moment for visitors when they arrive at Jurassic World's towering entrance. They know they are just moments away from getting their first glimpse of real, live dinosaurs! A large arched gateway with flaming torches welcomes them in.

RAPTOR PADDOCK

Owen is training young Raptors in the Raptor Paddock when Claire Dearing, the Assistant Manager at the park, gets in touch. "A baby Triceratops has escaped from the Gentle Giants Petting Zoo! Will you help me investigate?" Owen agrees. With the opening of the playground area due later, this is no day for disasters!

THERE'S A DINO BREAKOUT!

WHAT WILL YOU BUILD?
- Hurdle race track
- Treat box with compartments

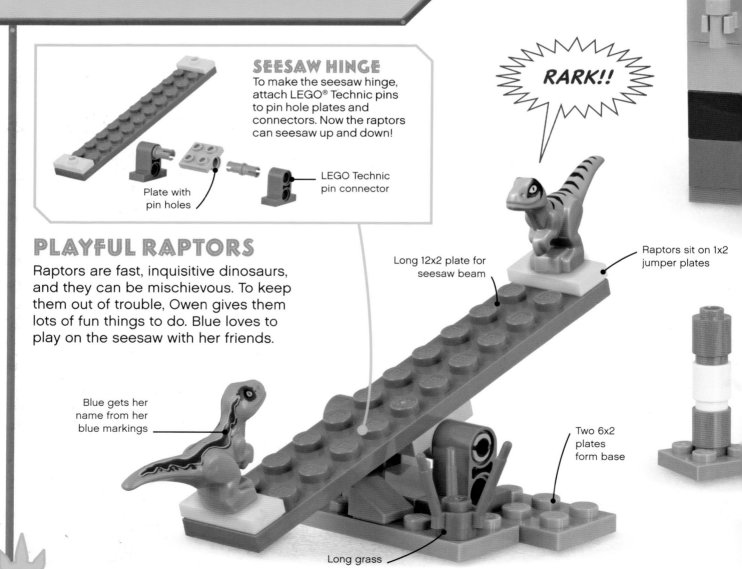

SEESAW HINGE
To make the seesaw hinge, attach LEGO® Technic pins to pin hole plates and connectors. Now the raptors can seesaw up and down!

Plate with pin holes

LEGO Technic pin connector

RARK!!

PLAYFUL RAPTORS
Raptors are fast, inquisitive dinosaurs, and they can be mischievous. To keep them out of trouble, Owen gives them lots of fun things to do. Blue loves to play on the seesaw with her friends.

Long 12x2 plate for seesaw beam

Raptors sit on 1x2 jumper plates

Blue gets her name from her blue markings

Two 6x2 plates form base

Long grass

RAPTOR TRAINING

It would be awkward if the Raptors pounced on a visitor for fun! To avoid this, Owen trains them to come when called. This Raptor training paddock shows three fences, but yours can have fences all the way around.

HEY, CLAIRE ... WHAT'S UP?

Light flashes when paddock gates open

Jurassic World colors

3x6 fence piece attached to clips

Long tiles reinforce brick wall

Brown 6x2 plate base

Plate with clip secures paddock fence

Brick with clip attached to brick with bar

RURK!

Red 1x1 round bricks make obstacle visible

Place the Raptors among the obstacles

Square plate base

SLALOM COURSE

Young Raptors love to run, so Owen has built a slalom course for them. Left, right, and left again they go, dodging the poles. Fastest Raptor gets a treat! Build some obstacles to add to the training paddock.

MAIN STREET

Owen and his dog, Red, set off to investigate. On the way to the Gentle Giants Petting Zoo, they pass through Main Street, a busy area filled with shops and stalls. The stallholder at the Dinosaur Bakery tells Owen that a box of doughnuts has gone missing overnight. Who could have taken it?

WHO'S THE DOUGHNUT THIEF?

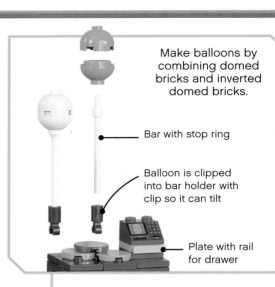

Make balloons by combining domed bricks and inverted domed bricks.

Bar with stop ring

Balloon is clipped into bar holder with clip so it can tilt

Plate with rail for drawer

STREET ENTERTAINER

That's no dinosaur—it's a street entertainer dressed up as one. Real dinosaurs don't juggle clubs while whistling pop tunes!

Clubs are ice-cream pieces on bars

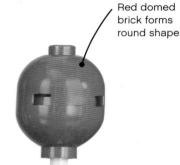

Red domed brick forms round shape

Slope with cash register print

Brown pieces for wooden stall

BALLOONS FOR SALE

Create a stall for visitors to buy colorful balloons. Be careful—if a balloon floats into a dinosaur paddock, you'll never get it back!

WHAT WILL YOU BUILD?

- A coffee stand
- Stall selling hats and other souvenirs

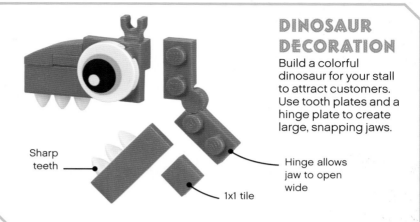

DINOSAUR DECORATION

Build a colorful dinosaur for your stall to attract customers. Use tooth plates and a hinge plate to create large, snapping jaws.

Sharp teeth

Hinge allows jaw to open wide

1x1 tile

BAKERY STALL

The bakery stall sells cupcakes, cookies, pies, and doughnuts. There will be a few disappointed customers today because some of the stock has been stolen!

SOMEONE HAS STICKY FINGERS ...

A BOX OF DOUGHNUTS HAS BEEN TAKEN!

Slope brick for back of stall

Large, watchful eye attracts attention

Dinosaur head attaches to a brick with side studs

Cakes and pastries for sale

VISITOR CENTER

After leaving Main Street, Owen and Red head to the Jurassic World Visitor Center. Could the baby Triceratops be hiding there? They jostle through the crowds, peeking among the dinosaur fossils and behind the interactive exhibits. But she isn't there. This is turning out to be quite a mystery!

WHAT'S GOING ON HERE?

The skull is built sideways using small white bricks.

Headlight brick on a jumper plate

Vertical tooth plate

Plate with bar

DINO SKULL

This massive dinosaur skull is a popular exhibit. It is from a fully grown Triceratops who lived a long time ago. It's much bigger than the missing baby dinosaur!

Interactive Triceratops info screen

IT'S OKAY ... I WORK HERE!

HEY! DON'T CUT IN LINE!

LEGO Technic axle is skull's pedestal

2x2 slope brick

LINE BARRIER

The Visitor Center gets busy, so people must wait behind a barrier until it is their turn to see the exhibits. Build a barrier with stacked round bricks and chains.

Sturdy base is a jumper plate

FOSSIL DISPLAY

Build a wall using bricks with clips or bricks with side studs that you can attach clip plates to. Then add white, bonelike pieces to create a dinosaur fossil shape.

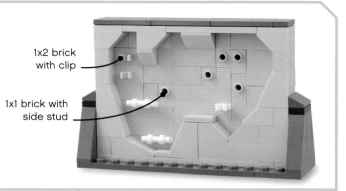

1x2 brick with clip

1x1 brick with side stud

WHAT WILL YOU BUILD?

- Pteranodon wing
- T. rex jaws
- Fossilized nest

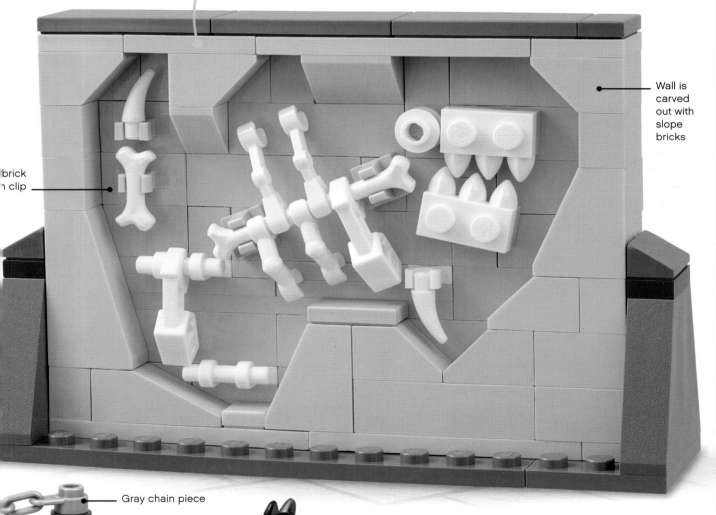

Wall is carved out with slope bricks

...brick ...clip

Gray chain piece

FOSSIL WALL

A dinosaur skeleton looks spectacular posed against a fossil wall. This one is a large carnivore with sharp teeth. What dinosaur fossil will you display on your wall?

17

TRICERATOPS PEN

Next, Owen and Red investigate the Gentle Giants Petting Zoo. In this popular attraction, young visitors can feed baby herbivores. Owen finds the Triceratops pen securely locked. That's odd! The baby Triceratops couldn't have closed and locked the gate after it escaped. So who did?

IT'S ALL A GIANT MYSTERY!

WHAT WILL YOU BUILD?
- Carrot delivery buggy
- Dinosaur saddle for visitors to ride on

6x5 plant leaves with studs

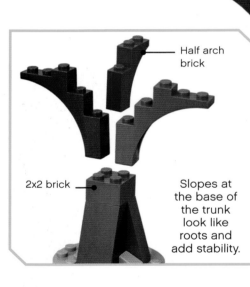

Half arch brick

2x2 brick

Slopes at the base of the trunk look like roots and add stability.

Half arch brick forms tree branch

Carrots for herbivore baby dinosaurs

TREE WITH BIRDS

Under the tree at the petting zoo visitors can collect carrots to feed to the baby dinosaurs. Build a tree with plenty of leaves with studs so that birds can perch on it.

6x6 round plate

Crate with handles

18

Bird perched on branch

BABY DINO ENCLOSURE

At least the other baby Triceratops is still safely in the pen! Construct a pen yourself with a secure fence, locking system, a hazard symbol, and a warning light in case of emergency. Don't forget to add some food, too.

Ladder pieces with clips at one end are perfect for making a rectangular pen.

Gate post

Ladder piece with clips

GOOD MORNING, GIRL!

2x2 brick joins top and bottom of tree

CRRW!

Dirt-colored plates

Digital keypad gate lock

SORRY, RED, IT'S FOR THE DINOS!

A VISIT TO THE LAB

At the Hammond Creation Lab, Owen meets with Claire and lead scientist Dr. Wu. It seems there is more trouble at the park. Danny Nedermeyer, the IT technician, was furious when he had to stay late to fix the computer system the night before. Then some eggs somehow got swapped in the incubator.

WHO MOVED THE EGGS?

DNA EXTRACTOR

The lab is named after John Hammond, the park's creator. He and Dr. Wu discovered how to create dinosaurs using their DNA. The DNA was extracted from prehistoric blood-sucking insects trapped in amber.

Bulb piece

1x1 round plate with hole

Short cone

2x2 round plate

Stacked round pieces suggest a machine that spins samples to extract DNA.

SCIENTIST'S DESK

This scientist's desk has a computer for recording information and jars to keep specimens in for study. You can build a computer screen that tilts using hinge bricks.

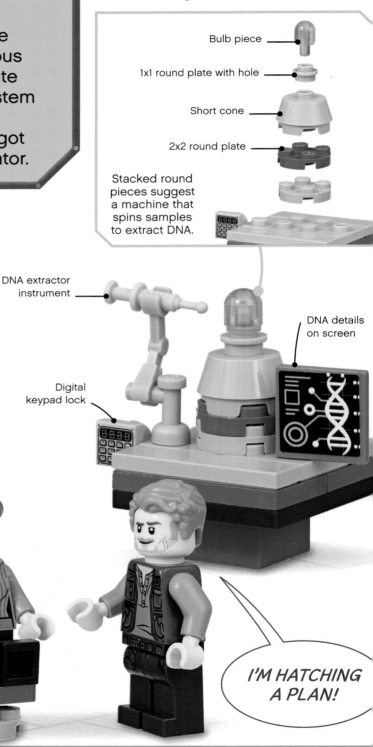

Computer screen tile

Hinge brick base for screen to rotate on

DNA extractor instrument

Digital keypad lock

DNA details on screen

WHAT'S THE NEWS?

I'M HATCHING A PLAN!

2x2 round plate is chair's base

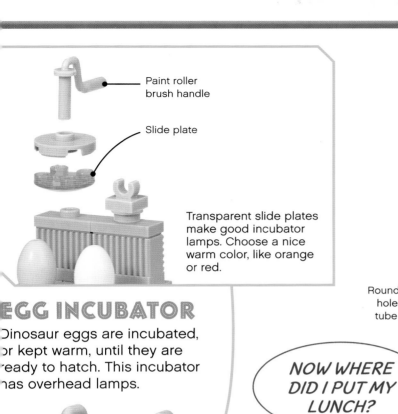

Paint roller brush handle

Slide plate

Transparent slide plates make good incubator lamps. Choose a nice warm color, like orange or red.

Half cylinder

LEGO Technic half pin

Use pins to look like rivets around the top and bottom of the freezer.

EGG INCUBATOR

Dinosaur eggs are incubated, or kept warm, until they are ready to hatch. This incubator has overhead lamps.

Round plates with holes are freeze tube connectors

NOW WHERE DID I PUT MY LUNCH?

Eggs rest on 2x2 jumper plates

Sturdy base in Jurassic World blue colors

Round brick with holes

Plate with clip

DNA FREEZER

The lab has a container for freezing dinosaur DNA. One of the scientists, Allison Miles, is using it today.

CONTROL ROOM

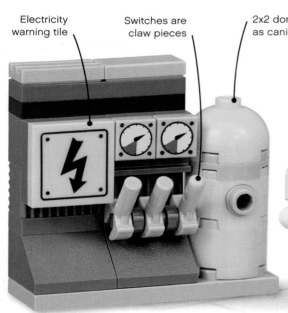

Entering the park's Control Room, Owen and Claire are greeted by security chief Vic Hoskins. "It seems the baby dinosaur's tracking device has been taken off," Vic says. Someone has spotted a trail of doughnut scraps leading from Main Street to the Baryonyx Feeding Arena, too. Hmm ...

I'M IN CONTROL HERE!

DINOSAUR TRACKER

The Control Room staff can see the location of the dinosaurs on a large screen—as long as a dinosaur is fitted with a tracking device!

Window piece with Jurassic World map print

Plate with clip holds screen in place

Gray slope piece looks like smooth metallic surface

Electricity warning tile

Switches are claw pieces

2x2 dome used as canister top

WE'VE GOT TO TRACK IT DOWN!

Vic Hoskins's computer

Large coffee mug

POWER LOCKS

The locks on the dinosaur paddocks are powered by electricity. This electrical unit has switches, a danger symbol, and dials showing power voltage.

Tile with computer keyboard print

SECURITY MONITORS

Danny, the IT technician, has been fixing the park's computer system. Build some computer monitors, keyboards, and screens for the Control Room.

Bar holder with clip attached to plate with bar

Round, colored tiles look like lights. They attach to LEGO Technic half pins that plug into a brick with holes.

LEGO Technic pin with bar

1x1 transparent round tile

Brick with holes

Inverted radar dish

Bar holder with handle

Gray bar

REAR VIEW

1x8 tile makes neat panel top

Lights flash in an emergency

NOT ANOTHER BREAKOUT!

Map of Jurassic World

Walkie-talkie

From his seat, Danny can see all the park's activity

CHAPTER 2
FEEDING TIME

BARYONYX ARENA

It's feeding time at the Baryonyx Arena down by the river, but strangely, the dinosaur isn't hungry for her fish today. Could the doughnut scraps lying by the fence have something to do with that? There's still no sign of the baby Triceratops, either. Owen hopes she's not in the Baryonyx's stomach!

SOMETHING'S FISHY HERE!

DINOSAUR FEEDER

Even the bravest keeper wouldn't dare to feed a Baryonyx by hand! Build a tall crane with a control cab and a long arm so he can pass fish to the sharp-toothed dinosaur without venturing too close.

Plates with clips form tilting lights

MAYBE WITH SOME RELISH?

Yellow, stripy hazard tile

Brick with cross axle hole holds antenna piece

Antenna looks like fence bar

CONTROL CAB

Build a control cab with a turntable for a base so that it can swivel. Use plates with bars and plates with clips to make a bendable arm.

1x2 plate with bar

4x4 round plate

Turntable base piece

WHAT A MESSY EATER!

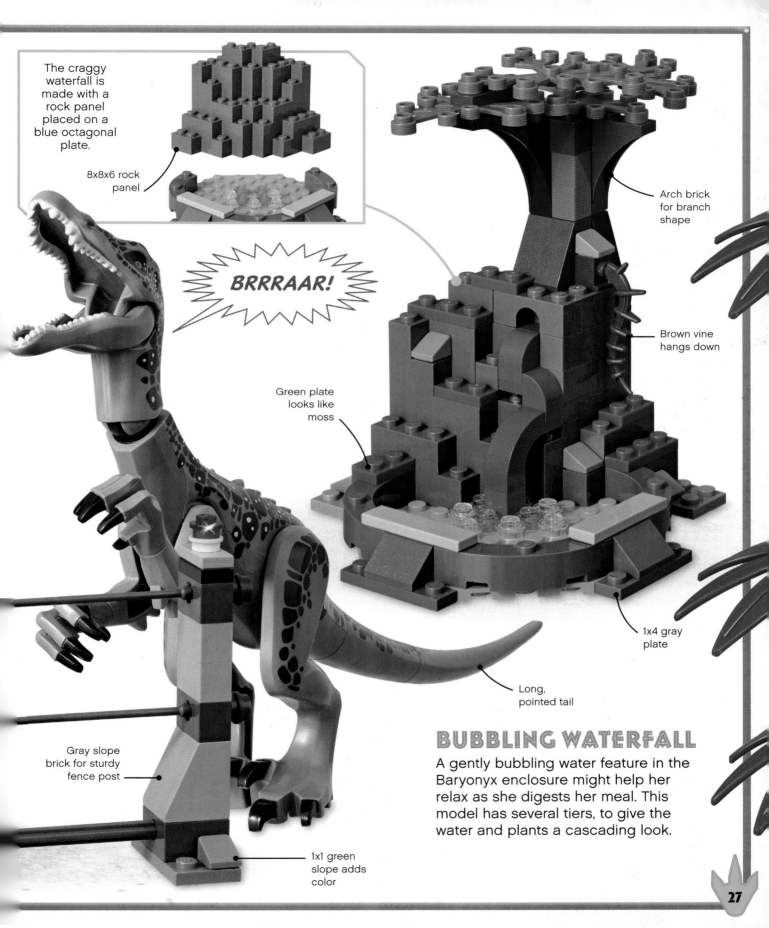

The craggy waterfall is made with a rock panel placed on a blue octagonal plate.

8x8x6 rock panel

Arch brick for branch shape

Brown vine hangs down

BRRRAAR!

Green plate looks like moss

1x4 gray plate

Long, pointed tail

Gray slope brick for sturdy fence post

1x1 green slope adds color

BUBBLING WATERFALL

A gently bubbling water feature in the Baryonyx enclosure might help her relax as she digests her meal. This model has several tiers, to give the water and plants a cascading look.

STRANGE FOOTPRINTS

Where can that baby Triceratops have gone? Owen and Red hop into a boat at the jetty and travel downriver toward the lake. There they find footprints in the mud, but they're too big to be the baby's. In fact, the footprints don't look like they were made by any of the park's dinosaurs!

SOMETHING STRANGE IS AFOOT!

WHAT A COOL VIEW!

Tile printed with map pattern

Brown tiles are planks

LET'S STEP ON IT!

Antenna for tracking boat's route

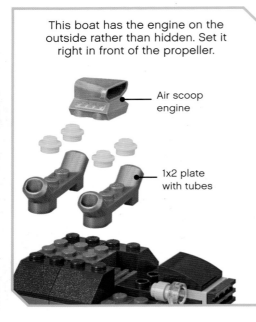

This boat has the engine on the outside rather than hidden. Set it right in front of the propeller.

Air scoop engine

1x2 plate with tubes

SPEEDBOAT

Owen's speedboat is small but powerful, so include a really large propeller at the back. Add a pair of movable joysticks at the front for Owen to steer the boat with.

Radar web dish is back of propeller

Slopes form sides of boat

Blue flag blows
in wind

BOAT JETTY

A jetty is a structure for boats
to land at or launch from.
Build yours from brown bricks
and plates to look like wood.
Don't forget a map of the
waterways, and a life buoy!

Light indicates
boat is departing

Life buoy

Choppy water

Bubbles form
at jetty supports

RIVERBANK

The plants in this build are in sludgy green
and off-white shades. They include curly
grasses and prickly bushes—just the sort
of plants that might grow on a muddy
riverbank where the woods begin.

Sword leaves make
a shady canopy

Layers of leaves
slide onto bar

Flower plate

Curly grass stem

Prickly bush
growing in
the mud

Bar to attach leaves

LEGO Technic
axle and pin
connector

LEGO
Technic axle

2x2 round
brick

GROW A
WOODLAND TREE

To make a twisting, turning
tree trunk like this one,
use angled LEGO® Technic
axle and pin connectors
attached in opposite
directions. A round brick
makes the base.

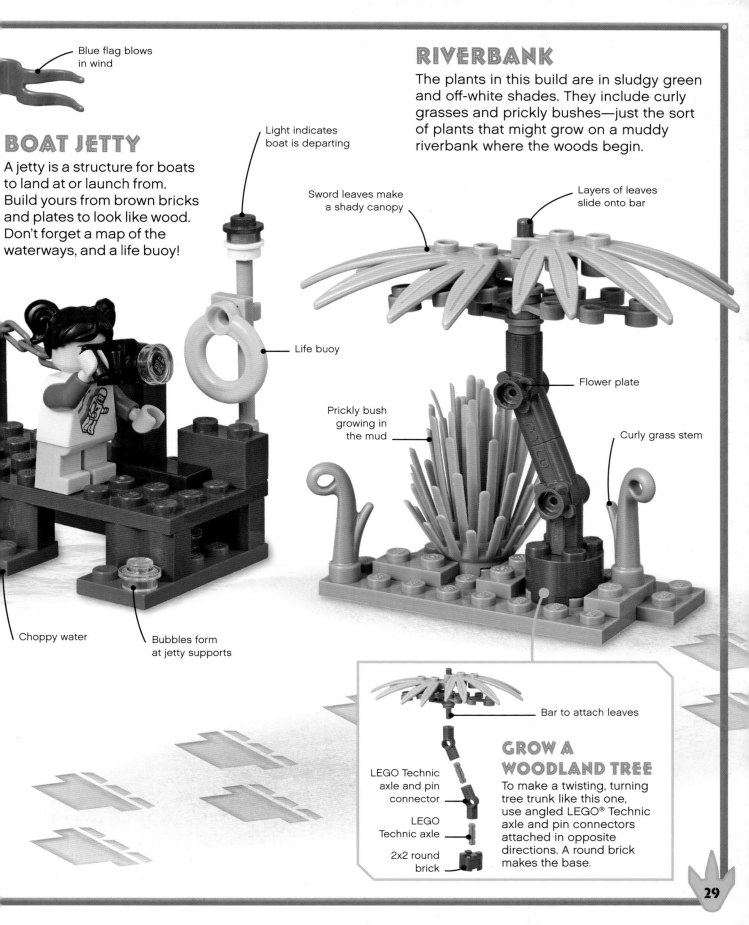

GYROSPHERE VALLEY

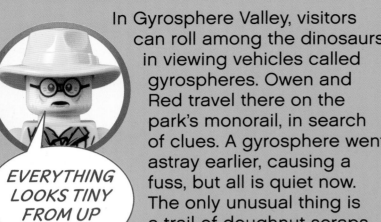

In Gyrosphere Valley, visitors can roll among the dinosaurs in viewing vehicles called gyrospheres. Owen and Red travel there on the park's monorail, in search of clues. A gyrosphere went astray earlier, causing a fuss, but all is quiet now. The only unusual thing is a trail of doughnut scraps.

EVERYTHING LOOKS TINY FROM UP HERE!

WHAT WILL YOU BUILD?
- Miniature T. rex paddock
- Miniature Hammond Creation Lab

RAPTOR PADDOCK

The monorail glides overhead, giving breathtaking views over the entire park. Make some miniature builds of things visitors might see, including the Raptor Paddock. It should have high walls and rails to keep those lively Raptors in!

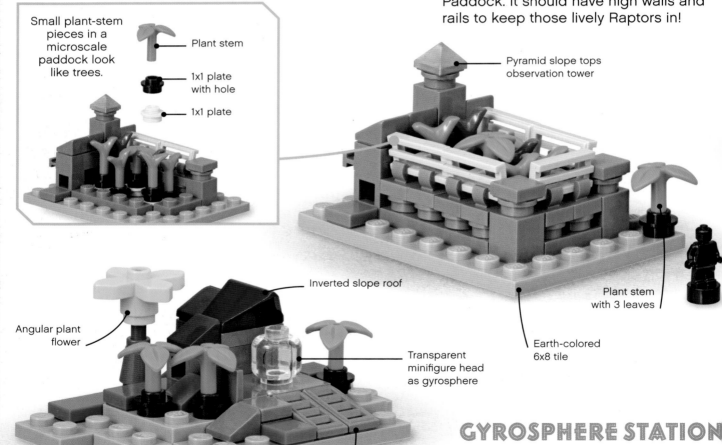

Small plant-stem pieces in a microscale paddock look like trees.

Plant stem

1x1 plate with hole

1x1 plate

Pyramid slope tops observation tower

Plant stem with 3 leaves

Earth-colored 6x8 tile

Inverted slope roof

Angular plant flower

Transparent minifigure head as gyrosphere

2 grille slopes

GYROSPHERE STATION

This is where visitors board the gyrospheres, which then roll down a ramp into a viewing enclosure. Invisible fence technology keeps the dinos in, so there's no need to build a barrier.

MICRO MONORAIL

all, graceful pillars support the
ack for the monorail. Give
n impression of its height by
urrounding it with trees that look
hort in comparison. The train
self can be several coaches long.

PLATE TRAIN

Build the high-tech monorail with a series
of 1x1 plates attached to a jumper plate.
The transparent plates look like windows.

Transparent
1x1 plate

Jumper plate

Lush, tropical
vegetation

1x1 tile attaches
to headlight brick

Leaves in various
shades of green

Brick arch

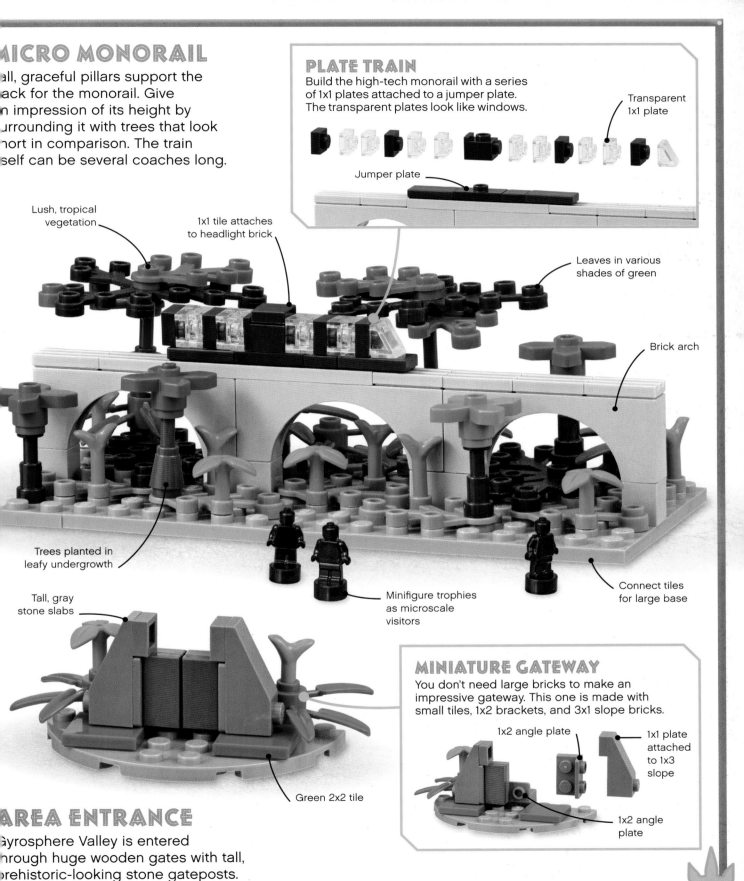

Trees planted in
leafy undergrowth

Minifigure trophies
as microscale
visitors

Connect tiles
for large base

Tall, gray
stone slabs

MINIATURE GATEWAY

You don't need large bricks to make an
impressive gateway. This one is made with
small tiles, 1x2 brackets, and 3x1 slope bricks.

1x2 angle plate

1x1 plate
attached
to 1x3
slope

Green 2x2 tile

1x2 angle
plate

AREA ENTRANCE

Gyrosphere Valley is entered
hrough huge wooden gates with tall,
prehistoric-looking stone gateposts.

A STRAY GYROSPHERE

Something behind a rock catches Owen's eye. It's the baby Triceratops ... and the lost gyrosphere! Nearby is Hudson Harper, a young dinosaur fan. "I found her at the end of a trail of crumbs," he says. "Then we went for a ride!" Owen sees that the sphere is damaged. Did a larger dinosaur do that?

I WAS GOING TO TAKE HER BACK!

WHAT WILL YOU BUILD?
- Gyrosphere parking
- Snack booth

1x1 slope brick for top of rocky crag

ROCKY OUTCROP

Owen and Red find the baby Triceratops hidden behind a large boulder. Add to your Jurassic World landscape by building some rocky crags. This one has a 3x8x7 gray rock panel as a base.

1x1 round plate

Large rock piece is base for build

Blue plate with gear teeth looks like water

WE SHARED THE LAST DOUGHNUT!

Gyrosphere is from a LEGO® Jurassic World™ set

URASSIC TREES

he herbivore dinosaurs are right at home among
he trees and shrubs of Gyrosphere Valley. The
ranches of lush leaves provide plenty to
unch on or to shelter under. Build
ome trees of all different shapes
nd some pools of water to
rink from, too.

LEGO Technic axle
and pin connector

2x2 round
brick with
axle hole

Palm tree leaf

Round brick
with four hooks

Create a palm-tree
shape using a brick
with hooks and green
palm leaves.

Plants grow in
between rocks

MMGH!

Gray slope brick
makes a great
rocky edge

Leafy crag for
Gyrosphere
Valley
landscape

SO THE BABY
DINO STOLE THE
DOUGHNUTS!

CHAPTER 3
PTERANODON ESCAPE

OWEN'S TRAILER

Owen escorts Hudson to safety and takes the Triceratops for a health check. Time for a breather at last! But as he chats to Claire in the trailer, more news comes in. Some Pteranodons have escaped from The Aviary—and it's not long until the grand opening of the playground area!

NO TIME FOR A REST!

Chimney attaches to range hood

The sleeping area is a half of an old-fashioned trailer, complete with colored horizontal band.

Curved slope

Cozy checkered quilt

Attach back wall to end of bed

LEGO® Technic axle and pin connector

Lattice window pane

Jumper plate for drawer front

IS THAT THE CONTROL ROOM?

Log bricks for the cabin section

Trailer walls are curved

Trailer is parked on grassy patch

REAR VIEW

Long red
slopes look
like roof tiles

Wall-
mounted
screen

Plate with ring

LEGO
Technic
T-bar

Make a TV aerial
by connecting
T-shaped bar
pieces and
attach it to a
plate with ring.

Sloped roof

Pizza for
midnight
snacks

Trailer
tow hitch

Wheels on
connector
pegs

Bricks to help
stabilize trailer

YES ... THEY
NEED US AGAIN!

LIVING QUARTERS

Owen's small trailer has just
enough room for a bed, stove,
and table. This model includes
a wall-mounted screen, so Owen
can communicate with park staff
and watch TV when off duty.

HELICOPTER LAUNCH

Owen races to the helicopter pad. Maybe he can better assess the situation from the air. He takes Blue along to assist him. "We must find those Pteranodons quickly," shouts Claire as Owen takes off. "We don't want any trouble at the opening of the new playground area!"

CAN'T STOP ... GOT TO FLY!

For an eye-catching radar dish mast, attach a bar to a minifigure's ray blaster.

Bar

Ray blaster

Antenna whip

Small radar dish on bar

WHAT WILL YOU BUILD?
- Hangar
- Cargo baskets
- Tow cart

LAUNCH EQUIPMENT

For safety's sake, the helicopter must not take off until Owen receives the all clear from the air traffic control tower. This ATC tower has several radar dishes and a tall antenna to monitor the sky for any airborne hazards.

2x2x10 triangular support girder

Brightly colored domed bricks and round bricks make up the fuel tanks.

Tap

Round brick with pin holes

Aviation fuel tanks

Scrubby plants grow near airfield

Spiky grasses

Helicopter rotor has a click hinge clip

Radar dish

Tail rotor

Flip-down cockpit is a windshield with handle

I NEED A PTERANODON'S EYE VIEW!

Helicopter sled rails

QUAA!

16x16 plate

The helicopter takes off in line with the "H"

Hazard stripes

2x2 bricks support corners

GOOD LUCK, OWEN!

HELIPAD

The helicopter launchpad has to be clearly visible from the air. Use bright red tiles on gray to spell out a nice clear "H," and add hazard stripes to define the edges.

UP IN THE AIR

High above the park, Owen and Blue are searching the skies when a hot-air balloon floats into view. Its pilot looks a little nervous, and no wonder. Some lively young Pteranodons are trying to play with the balloon! A cluster of camera drones hovers nearby, taking video footage from the air.

I'VE GOT HIGH HOPES!

SECURITY DRONES

Drones are small, pilotless craft that fly by remote control. The Asset Containment Unit (ACU) launches its fleet of drones to find and photograph any unusual goings-on in park airspace.

Propeller

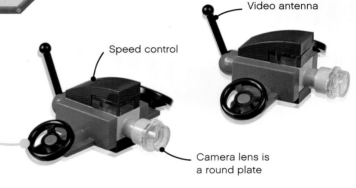

Video antenna

Speed control

Camera lens is a round plate

TINY FLIERS

These tiny drones are made up of a few small parts. Gather your small LEGO pieces and look for any that could be used as propellers, lights, and so on.

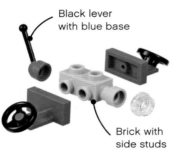

Black lever with blue base

Brick with side studs

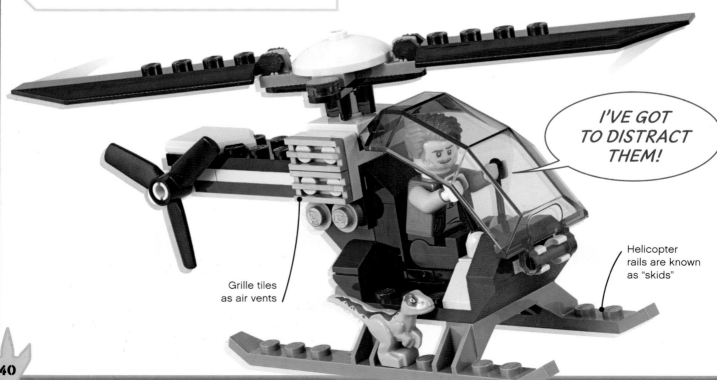

I'VE GOT TO DISTRACT THEM!

Helicopter rails are known as "skids"

Grille tiles as air vents

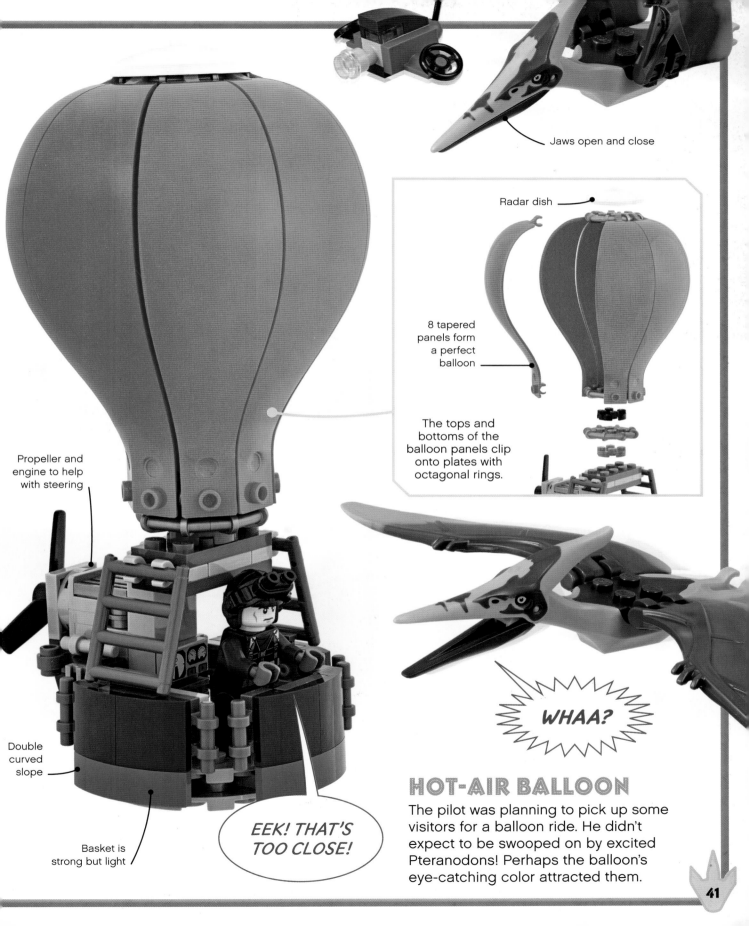

Jaws open and close

Radar dish

8 tapered
panels form
a perfect
balloon

The tops and
bottoms of the
balloon panels clip
onto plates with
octagonal rings.

Propeller and
engine to help
with steering

Double
curved
slope

Basket is
strong but light

*EEK! THAT'S
TOO CLOSE!*

WHAA?

HOT-AIR BALLOON

The pilot was planning to pick up some
visitors for a balloon ride. He didn't
expect to be swooped on by excited
Pteranodons! Perhaps the balloon's
eye-catching color attracted them.

THE AVIARY

Luckily, Owen has a large chicken drumstick with him. He was about to eat lunch when the call for help came! Owen attaches it to the outside of the helicopter to coax the Pteranodons away from the hot-air balloon. Soon, all the Pteranodons are safely back in their aviary.

FEELING PECKISH?

WATER TABLE

After their adventure with the balloon and the security drones, the Pteranodons are thirsty. Build a water table for them with transparent and blue plates attached to a radar dish.

WHAT WILL YOU BUILD?
- Treat containers
- Pteranodon exercise frame

FLIPPED FOUNTAIN

The top half of the water table is built upside down. The two halves are connected by a LEGO Technic axle.

1x2 plates attach water to dish

LEGO Technic axle

Upside-down round plate with hole

2x2 brick with hole

Fountain sits on 4x4 plate

TWEET!

Transparent slide plates on blue plates look like water

Spiky green leaves

Birds gather at the water table

Brown plates for sturdy base

FRWWW!

Green leaves of differing colors

EGG NEST

A Pteranodon has laid some eggs in The Aviary—and one of them has hatched! Make a cozy nest with LEGO eggs, a round plate, and leaf pieces connected in a circular shape.

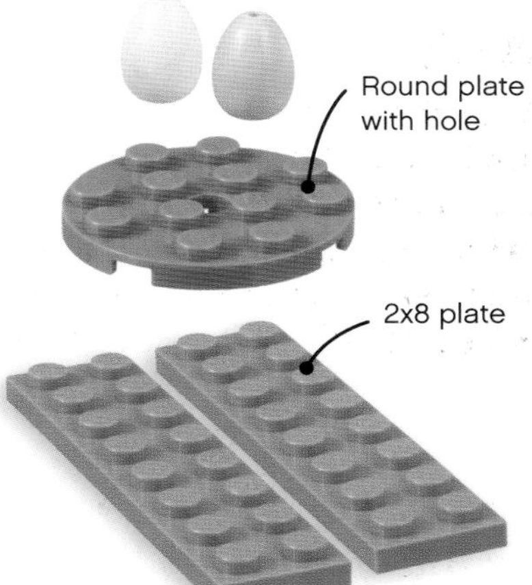

Round plate with hole

2x8 plate

Half arch

NEST BASE

The base of the nest is actually very simple to build. Attach leaf pieces to the base in a circle to give it a round shape and leafy appearance.

Green flower piece

Leaf piece

TREE WITH PERCHES

The Pteranodons love to soar and glide, but they also love a place to perch for a rest. Build a comfy tree perch with branches at different levels.

MEDICAL CENTER

Next, Owen visits the Medical Center to check on the baby Triceratops. At the center, dinosaur doctors, called Paleoveterinarians, look after sick and injured dinosaurs. They have checked the baby Triceratops and she is fine. She's now fast asleep after her tiring adventure!

WE'RE THE DINO DOCTORS!

WHAT WILL YOU BUILD?

- Operating table
- Medicine cabinet
- Dino snack cart

Transparent yellow slide plate looks like light

A plate with handle and two 1x1 slopes give lamp its shape

BRIGHT IDEA

The medical examination lamp has a plate with handle that attaches to a clip. This means that it can be angled as needed.

1x2 plate with handle

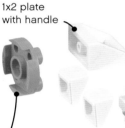

2x2 round plates connect lamp elements

Plate with clip sits on pole

1x1 cone

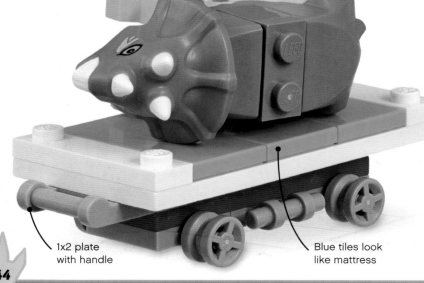

Plates are white—clinical and clean

Radar dish makes a sturdy base

1x2 plate with handle

Blue tiles look like mattress

GURNEY AND LAMP

Build a wheeled gurney for sick dinosaurs to rest on. An adjustable light allows the Paleoveterinarian to examine them closely.

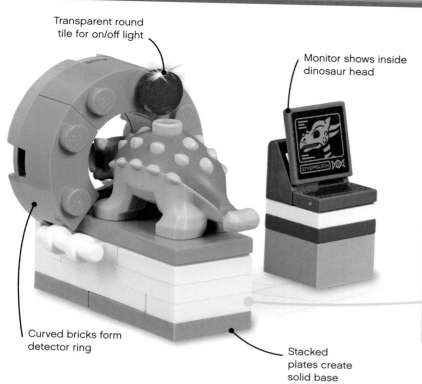

Transparent round tile for on/off light

Monitor shows inside dinosaur head

Curved bricks form detector ring

Stacked plates create solid base

CT SCANNER

Baby dinosaurs love a little rough and tumble, so it's no surprise that they take the odd knock. This CT scanner creates pictures of the insides of dinosaur bodies to check for injuries.

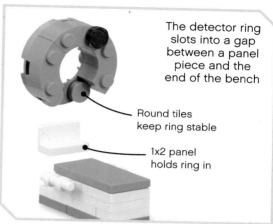

The detector ring slots into a gap between a panel piece and the end of the bench

Round tiles keep ring stable

1x2 panel holds ring in

MEDICINE CART

No medical center is complete without a cart to carry medicines and equipment. Build a cart where the Paleoveterinarian can keep syringes, bandages, a stethoscope, or bottles of medicine.

AH ... THE BABY DINO LOOKS SO COMFY

Syringe

Wheels and axle clip into round plate with holder

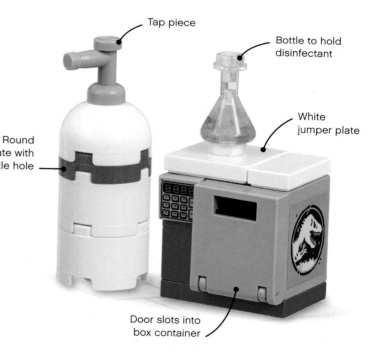

Tap piece

Bottle to hold disinfectant

White jumper plate

Round plate with axle hole

Door slots into box container

LABORATORY OVEN

This oven heats up medical equipment to sterilize it so it is free from germs. Build one with an opening door, a control panel, and a fire extinguisher by the side.

CHAPTER 4
A RAPTOR RESCUE

47

POWER GENERATOR

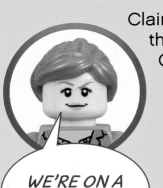

Claire and Owen wonder how the dinosaurs are escaping. Could an electrical fault be making the paddock gates open? They stop by the power generator and notice a fallen tree on the roof. Aha! But when they inspect the generator, they find it is still working perfectly. They will have to think again.

WE'RE ON A POWER TRIP!

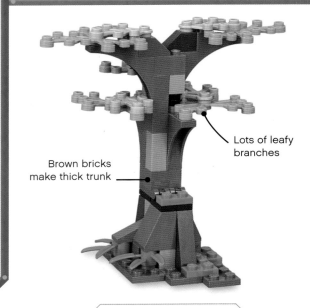

Lots of leafy branches

Brown bricks make thick trunk

UPRIGHT TREE

FALLEN TREE

Part of a large tree has blown over in a storm. Create a fallen tree using brown bricks of different shapes, half arch pieces, and leaf pieces. Make the tree any shape or size you like!

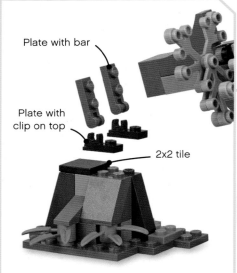

Plate with bar

Plate with clip on top

2x2 tile

BROKEN TRUNK

Use plates with bars on the upper part of the trunk and plates with clips on the bottom. The upper part will swing to the side, as if broken.

Mix of green and brown leaves

Tree has split in half

NO BROKEN CONNECTIONS HERE!

Gray slope piece looks like metal

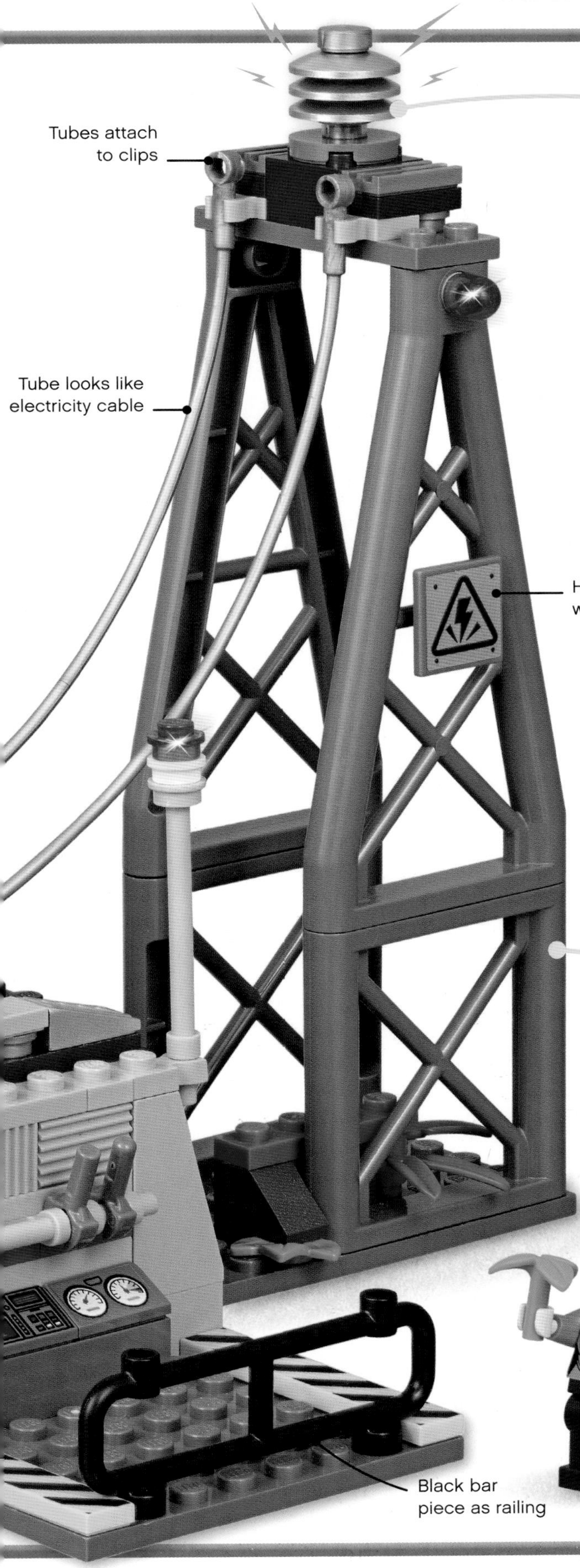

Tubes attach to clips

Tube looks like electricity cable

TOWER PROTECTION

Add a conductor at the top of the tower to protect the generator from lightning strikes. A stack of round pieces achieves this look.

1x1 round tile

2x2 radar dish

Round tile with open stud

1x2 grille

Hazard warning tile

GENERATOR TOWER

This generator supplies electricity for the whole park, including the paddock locks, so it needs to be in full working order. Build one with hazard symbols, dials, a control panel, cables, and a tall tower.

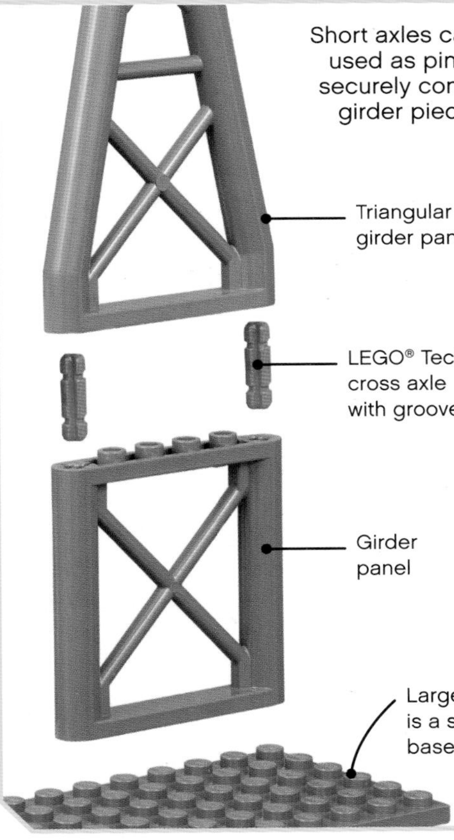

Short axles can be used as pins to securely connect girder pieces.

Triangular girder panel

LEGO® Technic cross axle with groove

Girder panel

Large plate is a sturdy base

Black bar piece as railing

OWEN'S WORKSHOP

Claire is worried. "What if the really big dinosaurs, like the Ankylosaurus, get out of their paddocks?" she asks. Claire and Owen look at each other. Then they rush to Owen's workshop! Owen jumps onto his motorcycle, with Blue in the sidecar, and Claire climbs into the dino mech.

INVENTIONS? ALL IN A DAY'S WORK!

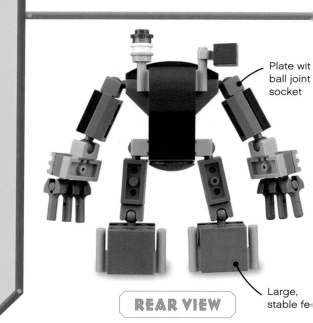

Plate wit ball joint socket

REAR VIEW

Large, stable fe

DINO MECH

For a tussle with a big dinosaur, you need a big dinosaur machine! Claire's mech combines modern technology with armorlike protective plates, fingers like Raptor claws, and stomping metal feet.

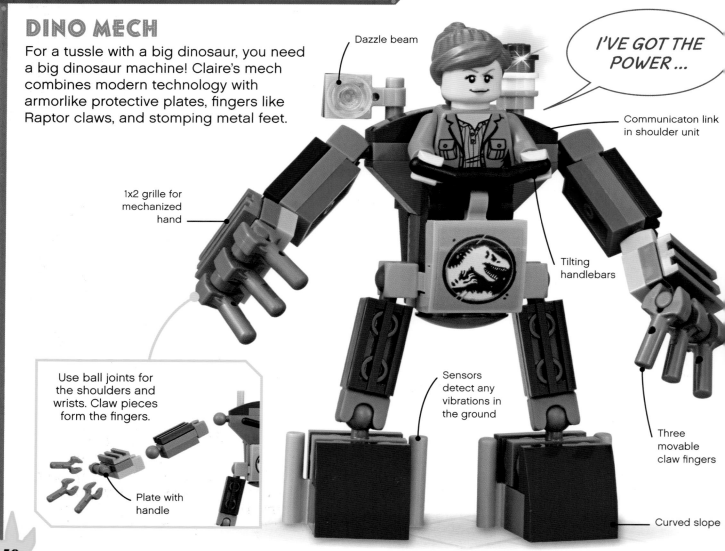

Dazzle beam

I'VE GOT THE POWER ...

Communicaton link in shoulder unit

1x2 grille for mechanized hand

Tilting handlebars

Use ball joints for the shoulders and wrists. Claw pieces form the fingers.

Plate with handle

Sensors detect any vibrations in the ground

Three movable claw fingers

Curved slope

TOOL KIT

Owen loves creating new things in his workshop, from safety clips to Raptor treat dispensers. Fix some clips to a wall so all his tools are in easy reach. You never know when inspiration will strike.

Long tiles for top of wall

Engine waiting to be fitted

Brown tiles for workbench planks

Wrench for adjusting bolts

Power drill

Anti-slip flooring in tool area

... AND I'VE GOT THE SPEED!

Fender shields rider from churned-up mud

Dirt bike fairing

Narrow, high-tread tires provide traction

Room for one in the sidecar!

WHAT WILL YOU BUILD?
- Baby dinosaur exercise wheel
- Shelves for storage

BIKE AND SIDECAR

Owen's motorcycle is specially built for off-road travel. It's meant to be super fast and light, so it does not have any details like big handlebars or baskets. Those things can slow a bike down!

A GREAT ESCAPE!

There's no sign of the enormous Ankylosaurus in its paddock. Owen lowers himself in for a closer look. Suddenly, the dino rears up from behind a tree! While Claire scrambles into the elevator to rescue Owen, the Ankylosaurus goes stomping out through the gates. They have been mysteriously unlocked!

DON'T PANIC!

STURDY PADDOCK

For a big Ankylosaurus, only the most secure paddock will do. This one is built from multiple girders and bars. It's fitted with alarms and warning lights, too. Anything to keep that Ankylosaurus in!

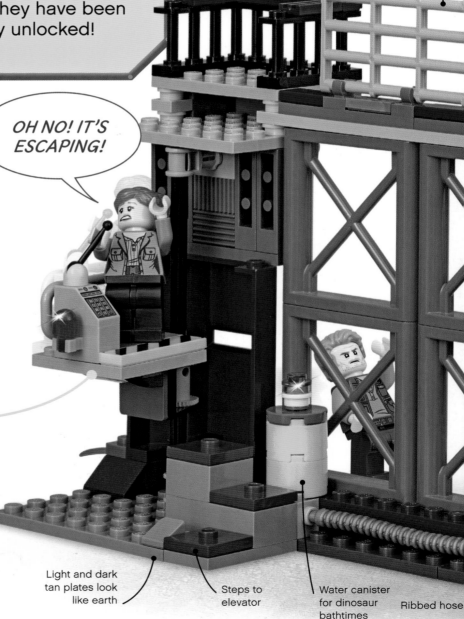

Observation platform

Bars add extra level of security

OH NO! IT'S ESCAPING!

WHAT WILL YOU BUILD?
- Mud bath for Ankylosaurus
- Alarm sirens

Control panel with joystick

String reel holder

Elevator travels on a LEGO Technic axle

GOING UP
The elevator is a simple platform with a digital control panel. It is attached to a reel holder, which slots onto a LEGO Technic axle.

Light and dark tan plates look like earth

Steps to elevator

Water canister for dinosaur bathtimes

Ribbed hose

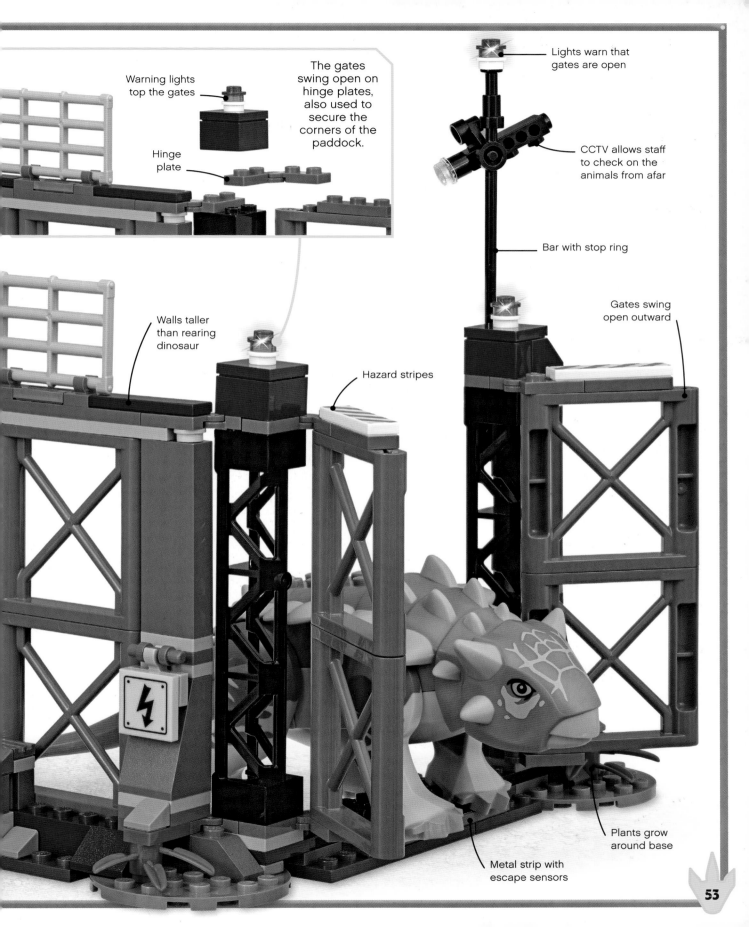

Warning lights top the gates

The gates swing open on hinge plates, also used to secure the corners of the paddock.

Hinge plate

Lights warn that gates are open

CCTV allows staff to check on the animals from afar

Bar with stop ring

Walls taller than rearing dinosaur

Hazard stripes

Gates swing open outward

Metal strip with escape sensors

Plants grow around base

THE WOODS

With the Ankylosaurus now on the loose, there's no time to waste! Owen takes his well-trained Raptors to track it down. They can sense things he can't. The Raptors find the Ankylosaurus in the woods. They jump out of the truck and start to run circles around it. In no time, it is totally disoriented!

LET'S GET TRUCKING!

RAPTOR TRUCK

Owen has hitched up a trailer to his truck for his Raptor passengers. It's best to make the trailer open so the Raptors can sniff the air for the scent of the Ankylosaurus as they go along.

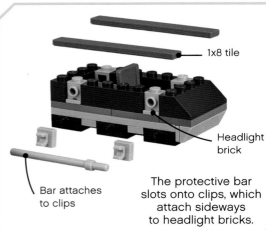

1x8 tile

Headlight brick

Bar attaches to clips

The protective bar slots onto clips, which attach sideways to headlight bricks.

The Raptor trailer attaches to a hook built into the back of the truck.

2x4 plate with hook

2x4 plate with hole

Torch clips to side of truck

I THINK WE'RE GETTING WARMER!

Raptor trailer has open sides

Blue is the color of Jurassic Park equipment

Clear panel windshield

Rugged tires for gripping muddy ground

The hood is a slope brick

These low-lying plant stems attach sideways to bricks with holes.

Leaves attach to LEGO Technic T-bar

1x2 brick with hole

RRR!

Leaf stem is dinosaur tail middle section

Spiky flower stem

Olive-green plant leaves

Three palm leaves on one stem

Dark-green plant vine

Plants fan out from central plate

Sword leaf with clip

A cone forms the base of low shrub

DEEPEST WOODS

The Ankylosaurus is hiding deep in the woods. This model uses leaves of many different sizes, colors, and shapes to suggest dense vegetation.

STRANGE ENCOUNTER

Suddenly, the entertainer in the dinosaur costume from Main Street runs past, chased by a Stygimoloch! The Raptors run off in alarm, but the Ankylosaurus doesn't. It charges straight at the Stygimoloch! Then both dinosaurs dash off into the undergrowth—toward the new playground area!

PEDAL TO THE METAL!

DAMAGED FENCING

The dino-costumed entertainer ducks under the fence to escape the Stygimoloch, but it crashes right through after him! Your model could show even more damage than this one if you like.

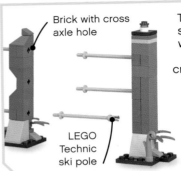

Brick with cross axle hole

The fence rails slot into bricks with holes and bricks with cross axle holes, built into the fence posts.

LEGO Technic ski pole

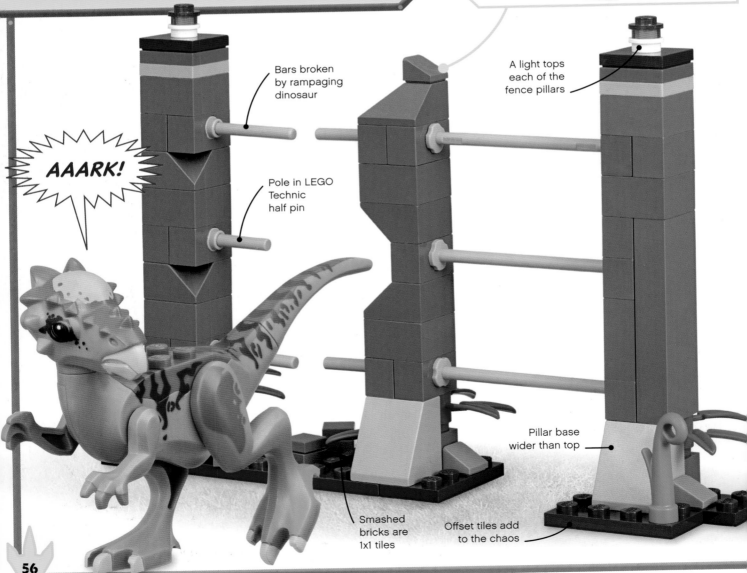

Bars broken by rampaging dinosaur

A light tops each of the fence pillars

AAARK!

Pole in LEGO Technic half pin

Pillar base wider than top

Smashed bricks are 1x1 tiles

Offset tiles add to the chaos

OKAY ...
DANGER'S OVER!

JURASSIC ROCKS

In the confusion, Owen crashes his truck into a tree and has to abandon it. He hides behind some rocks with the entertainer until the dinos are gone. Luckily, the rocks are big enough to hide both of them.

Plant leaves at base of rocks

Sludgy colors

1x2 plate with bar

1x1 plate with clip

The broken truck parts are attached with bars and clips, allowing them to be angled.

Slopes of different sizes

2x2x2 slope

Uneven, smashed-looking hood

Lights clip onto bar piece

Push bumper on plate with clips

TRASHED TRUCK

A Jurassic World truck was in the dinosaurs' path. It's a write-off! In this build, the truck is made in two halves Each end is propped up on bricks so the truck looks broken in the middle.

Tires all askew

Swampy ground

CHAPTER 5
A MYSTERY SOLVED

OLD PARK RUINS

There are two dinosaurs on the loose, both heading for the new playground area! Claire picks up Owen in her car, and they find the ruins of an old Jurassic Park building to shelter in. They have to make a plan—fast! Soon, Owen has an idea. He asks Claire to drive him to the T. rex paddock.

IT'S SAFE HERE, ISN'T IT?

WHAT WILL YOU BUILD?
• An ancient dinosaur paddock
• An old, broken computer

OLD PARK VEHICLE

Jurassic Park is an abandoned theme park from long ago. The ruins are spooky! Among them is an old off-roader, covered in plants. It has sunk into the mud and lost most of its wheels.

IT'S JUST A FOSSIL, GUYS!

Open studs make good perches for birds or small dinosaurs

Slope brick creates bent trunk effect

Yellow mudguard piece

Transparent 1x1 round plate looks like light

Sloped piece with camouflage print

Brown plates for sludgy mud

UURK?

ANCIENT WALL

A ruined wall from the original Jurassic Park entrance looks like it may have been trampled on by dinosaurs in the past. Now it's home to a big red spider in a cobweb.

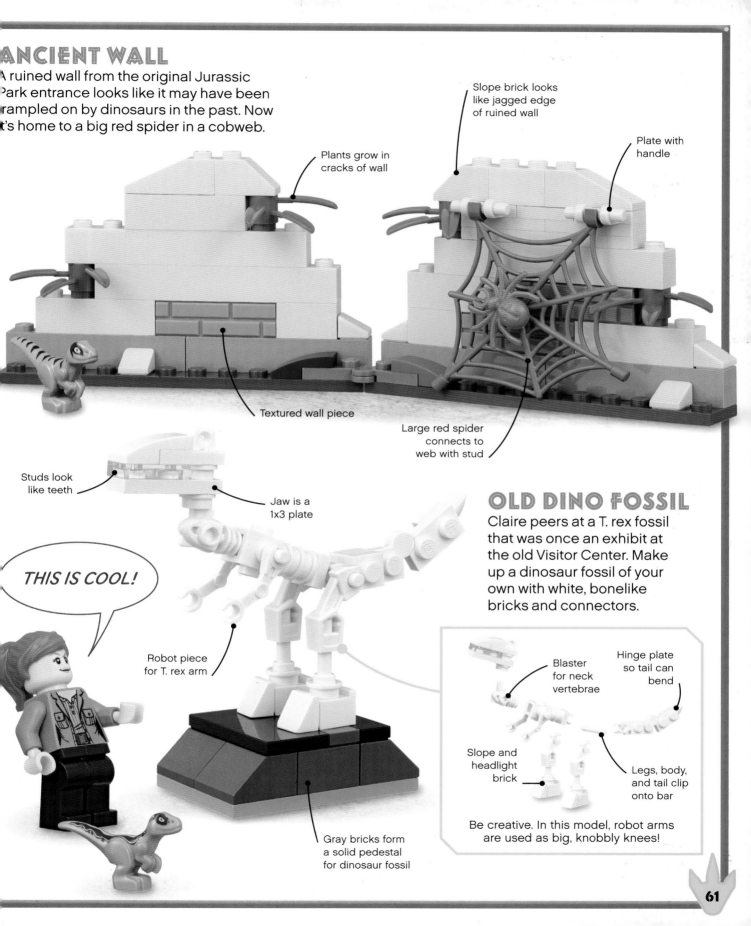

Slope brick looks like jagged edge of ruined wall

Plate with handle

Plants grow in cracks of wall

Textured wall piece

Large red spider connects to web with stud

Studs look like teeth

Jaw is a 1x3 plate

THIS IS COOL!

Robot piece for T. rex arm

Gray bricks form a solid pedestal for dinosaur fossil

OLD DINO FOSSIL

Claire peers at a T. rex fossil that was once an exhibit at the old Visitor Center. Make up a dinosaur fossil of your own with white, bonelike bricks and connectors.

Blaster for neck vertebrae

Hinge plate so tail can bend

Slope and headlight brick

Legs, body, and tail clip onto bar

Be creative. In this model, robot arms are used as big, knobbly knees!

A NEW PLAYGROUND

Over at the new playground area, excitement is growing. There are only minutes to go now until the grand opening! Somewhere in the crowd is little Hudson Harper, grinning away. Some of the visitors begin to nudge each other. Simon Masrani, the Jurassic World boss, has just arrived!

NOW THIS LOOKS LIKE FUN!

ROLLER COASTER

The new area has lots of exciting rides to thrill visitors. Build a tall roller coaster with tracks that swerve and curve. Just for fun, you could make one section look a little like a long-necked dinosaur!

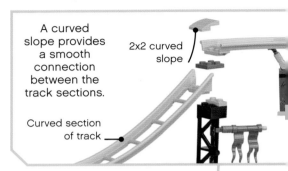

A curved slope provides a smooth connection between the track sections.

2x2 curved slope

Curved section of track

Add more sections until track forms a ring

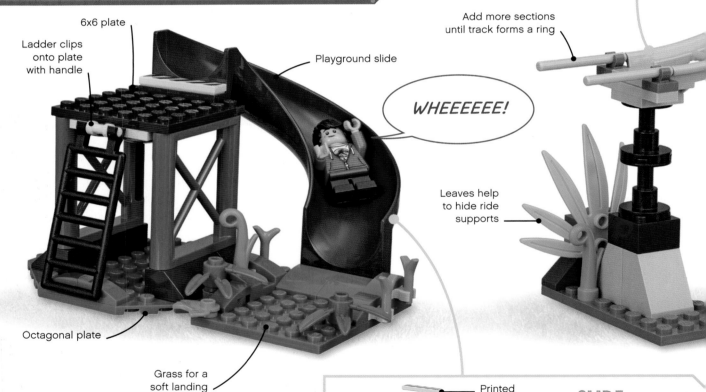

6x6 plate

Ladder clips onto plate with handle

Playground slide

WHEEEEEE!

Leaves help to hide ride supports

Octagonal plate

Grass for a soft landing

HIGH SLIDE

On this ride, visitors whiz down a curved slide leading from a platform on girder supports. Don't forget to add a ladder or some steps. Wheeeeeee!

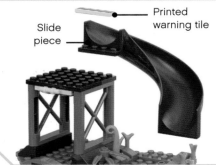

Slide piece

Printed warning tile

SLIDE SUPPORT

Build the platform to be the correct height for the slide piece to attach to. Add a printed tile to warn of a step up.

Bars keep riders
secure in seats

Car travels along
dinosaur's "back"

Curved slopes
make bumper

Sign clips
onto track

Track should
join up with
other end

Triangular
girders look like
dinosaur legs

Brightly colored
banners

TIME FOR
A SNACK!

Safety
information
sign

2 slope bricks

Ride spins on
a 4x4 round
brick and pin

JUST ONE MORE
SPIN, GUYS!

MERRY-GO-ROUND

Even the ACU likes to have
a little fun! This spinning
ride is quickly becoming a
visitor favorite. Since this is
a moving build, make the
base large, for stability,
then add the top section.

WHAT WILL YOU BUILD?

- Dino carousel
- Swing set
- Jungle gym

NO TIME TO LOSE!

Claire and Blue rush to the playground area to warn everyone that the dinosaurs are coming. They see Danny making final light and sound checks. They also see huge footprints like the ones in the woods. But as Claire starts to speak, the Ankylosaurus and Stygimoloch come crashing through the fence!

THIS JOB IS SUCH A HASSLE!

LIGHTS AND FLAGS

The preparations for the grand opening are nearly complete. Colorful flags are blowing in the wind, and floodlights have been put up to shine onto the stage.

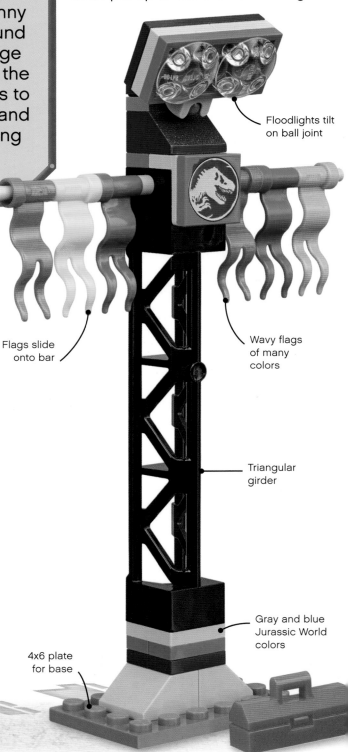

Floodlights tilt on ball joint

Wavy flags of many colors

Flags slide onto bar

Triangular girder

Gray and blue Jurassic World colors

4x6 plate for base

SUBWOOFER

A subwoofer is a big speaker that really pumps up the bass. For an impressive subwoofer, use your largest radar dish and set smaller dishes inside it. Then box the whole thing in with tiles.

Tiles box in large speakers for use on stage

2x2 radar dish inside 3x3 dish

CHERRY PICKER

Danny is operating a cherry picker so he can reach up high to check the floodlights. This cherry picker has two booms, but yours could have three—or even four—to reach really tall things.

BOOM TIME

Use LEGO® Technic friction pins to join the booms to each other and to the car and platform so you will be able to raise and lower the cherry picker.

Friction pin

Plate with a pin hole on top

WHAT WILL YOU BUILD?
• Microphone stand
• Podium for ribbon cutting

CAN'T YOU SEE I'M BUSY?

Antenna is control lever

Bar holder with clip keeps safety rail in place

Plate with hook

LEGO Technic lift arm

Tires with offset tread

DANNY... WE'VE GOT TO RUN!

LOUDSPEAKERS

There are speeches to be made, people to be thanked, and, of course, music to be played. A large array of loudspeakers is a must. Nobody in the crowd wants to miss a thing!

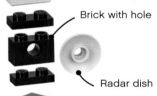

Include some jumper plates on your bench, to attach the speakers to.

Brick with hole

Radar dish

Jumper plate

Printed tile for mixing deck

Wrench for securing equipment

T. REX ALERT!

Seconds later, Owen crashes through the fence in his off-roader. A massive T. rex runs behind, gobbling up a trail of hot dogs leading from a crate on the vehicle. The two rampaging dinosaurs are so startled that they run back to their paddocks! Owen is careful to lead the T. rex back to her paddock, too.

DID SOMEONE SAY T. REX?

BUMPER BUILD

This bumper car has had more than a bump! To make your model look broken, attach parts to hinge bricks at crazy angles.

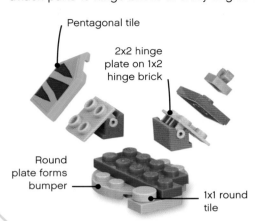

Pentagonal tile

2x2 hinge plate on 1x2 hinge brick

Round plate forms bumper

1x1 round tile

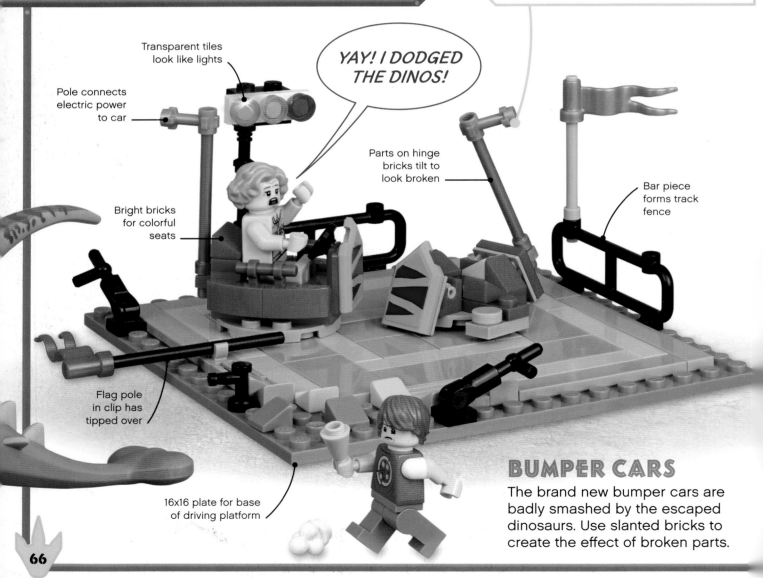

Transparent tiles look like lights

Pole connects electric power to car

YAY! I DODGED THE DINOS!

Parts on hinge bricks tilt to look broken

Bright bricks for colorful seats

Bar piece forms track fence

Flag pole in clip has tipped over

16x16 plate for base of driving platform

BUMPER CARS

The brand new bumper cars are badly smashed by the escaped dinosaurs. Use slanted bricks to create the effect of broken parts.

SECURITY FENCES

The Ankylosaurus and Stygimoloch even crash through the playground area's security fencing. It has only just been finished! Build fences that can easily be dismantled to look damaged.

ROOAAR!!

Round brick for alarm light

Plate with 2 studs

Rectangular girder panel

Don't connect girders to each other. You'll want to remove some and leave others standing.

Girder panel for strong fence

Yellow 1x1 round plates for fence alarms

Foliage from damaged tree

Crate with handles

Fence flattened by T. rex

A GRAND OPENING

Hooray! The grand opening can go ahead. Danny fixes the broken fence locks. Does he look a little shifty, or is it just Claire's imagination? Never mind that now! It's time to party, with music, food, and speeches. Owen and Claire are rocking out on stage. Danny is walking around on giant stilts!

I DECLARE THE PLAYGROUND AREA OPEN!

WHAT WILL YOU BUILD?

- Podium and lectern for speeches
- Soda fountain

HEY ... WHO TOOK THE LAST COOKIE?

WOOF!

I'M AS HUNGRY AS A T. REX!

Food items attach to exposed studs

Gauges show temperature

Grill raised on brick supports

Delicious cream-filled pie

Large, round tile forms table

BUILD A GRILL

Panel with rounded corners

For a sizzling grill, use red and orange round plates as smoldering charcoal. Set a couple of 1x2 grille tiles on top of them.

6x4 plate

PARTY FOOD

There are freshly grilled hot dogs and burgers to satisfy meat-loving visitors and baked goods (including doughnuts) to appeal to those with a sweet tooth.

Spotlight is a transparent slide plate

Light tilts on tow plate with ball joint

Tile with handle

Microphone on stand

LAAAA!

JURASSIC WORLD

Amplifier for guitar

Colorful diamond jewel pieces

LEGO Technic half pin

Diamond jewel piece

Long brick with holes

Pins act as sockets for light bulbs.

Plate with clip is a guitar stand

Step up to stage

MUSIC STAGE

This stage has a raised area with plenty of room for a band to rock out! A row of colored gems along the edge gives the look of a light show.

A MYSTERY SOLVED

Wait a minute, the footprints from Danny's stilts look just like the strange dino prints at the jetty. What has Danny been up to? It's time to find out! "Okay, okay, it was me!" admits Danny after Owen and Claire quiz him. "I was angry that I had to work late the other night to fix the computer system."

ARRGH! I NEARLY GOT AWAY WITH IT!

DINO STILTS

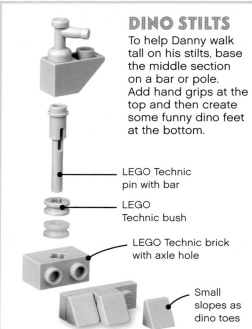

To help Danny walk tall on his stilts, base the middle section on a bar or pole. Add hand grips at the top and then create some funny dino feet at the bottom.

LEGO Technic pin with bar

LEGO Technic bush

LEGO Technic brick with axle hole

Small slopes as dino toes

THE END

Danny confesses to messing with the locking system to let the baby Triceratops and Pteranodons out, and to switching the eggs at the lab. "But I didn't mean to let the Ankylosaurus and Stygimoloch out!" he insists. "Oh, well! What's my punishment?"

CLEANING OUT THE DINO PADDOCKS ...

... FOR THE REST OF THE WEEK!

Tap with nozzle

DINO GLOSSARY

Almost every visitor who comes to Jurassic World has a "must-see" list of dinosaurs. Here are some of the most popular, exciting, and awe-inspiring dinosaurs in the park.

AND THEY WERE ALL CREATED BY ME!

VELOCIRAPTOR
ve-LOSS-ee-RAP-tor

Known as "Raptors" for short, these small, swift dinosaurs run in packs. Velociraptors have large brains, making them some of the most intelligent dinosaurs.

STYGIMOLOCH
STIJ-im-OH-lock

This dinosaur has a bony dome on her head, surrounded by rows of spikes. She can do a lot of damage if she decides to butt something!

ANKYLOSAURUS
an-KYE-lo-SAW-russ

This heavy plant eater is like a walking tank! Spikes and plates cover her body like armor. She defends herself by swinging her bone-tipped tail at enemies.

TRICERATOPS
tri-SERRA-tops

A Triceratops is easy to identify. She has three horns and a bony frill at the back of her head. This large plant eater will charge at anything she thinks is a threat.

PTERANODON
te-RAN-oh-don

A Pteranodon is not a dinosaur—she's a flying reptile. She has a long crest on the back of her head and skin-covered wings with a span of up to 18 ft (5.5 m).

BARYONYX
barry-ON-iks

A Baryonyx has a head like a crocodile's and a huge appetite for fish. She lurks in rivers, snatching fish from the water with her long arms and sharp claws.

TYRANNOSAURUS REX (T. REX)
ty-RAN-oh-SAW-russ reks

This huge, fast, meat eater is called T. rex for short. Her teeth are 1 ft (30 cm) long and give a very strong bite.

LEGO® size comparison chart

71

OWEN'S HELICOPTER

There are times when Owen has to go above and beyond his usual duties. In emergency situations, a helicopter enables him to survey multiple areas of the park all at once, then land just where he is needed. Build your own helicopter and take Owen up and away on a Jurassic World adventure.

Tranquilizer dart holder

ALTERNATIVE VIEW

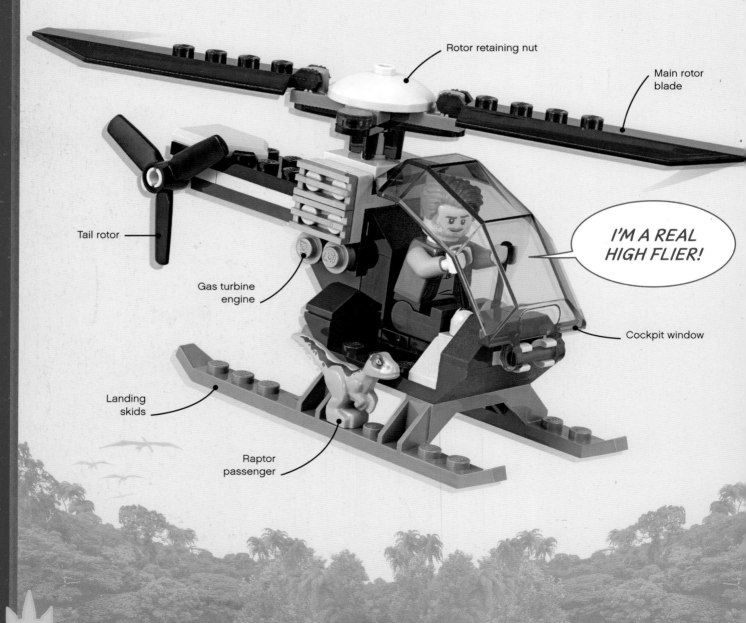

Rotor retaining nut

Main rotor blade

Tail rotor

Gas turbine engine

I'M A REAL HIGH FLIER!

Cockpit window

Landing skids

Raptor passenger

HELICOPTER INSTRUCTIONS

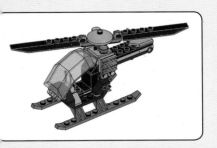

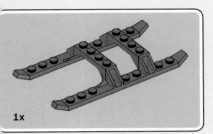

1x

1

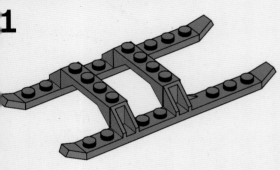

1x

2

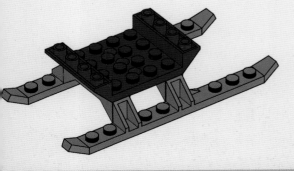

1x 1x 1x 1x

3

1x

4

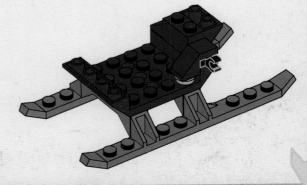

5

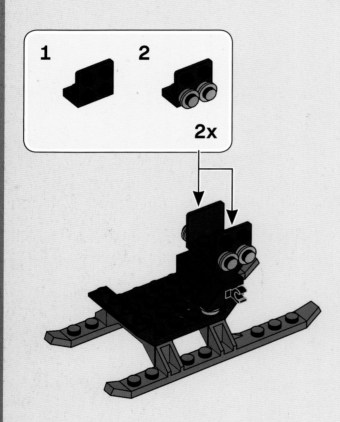

1 **2**

2x

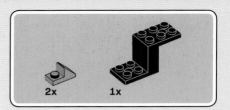

6

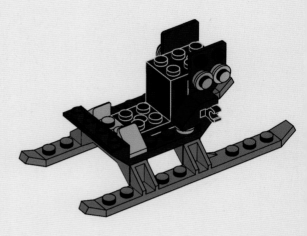

1x   1x

7

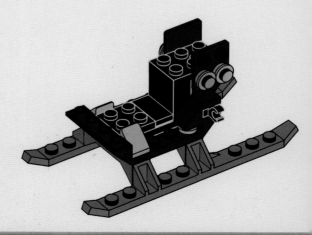

8

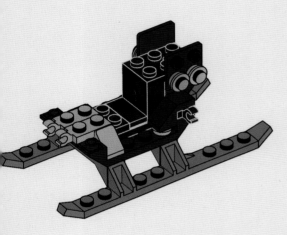

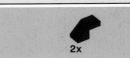

10

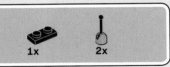

9

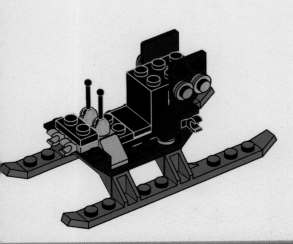

11

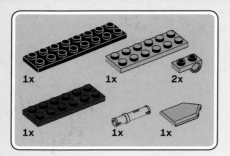

12

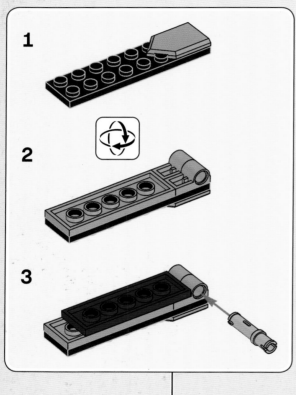

1

2

3

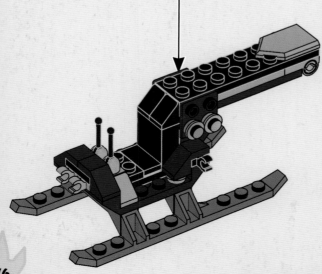

13

14

2x   4x

1   2

2x

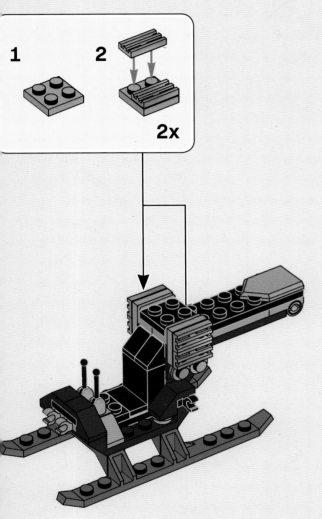

16

1x   1x

17

1x

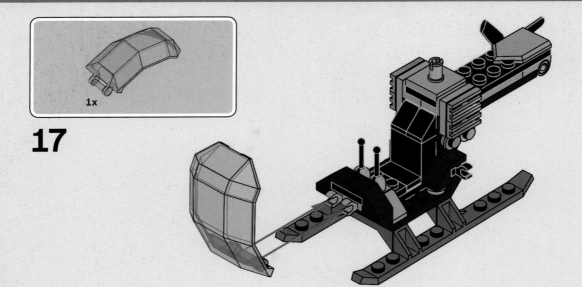

18

1x 2x 1x 1x

1x 2x

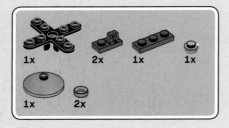

1

2

3

4

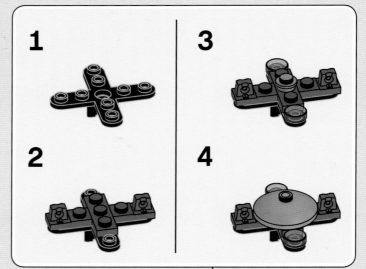

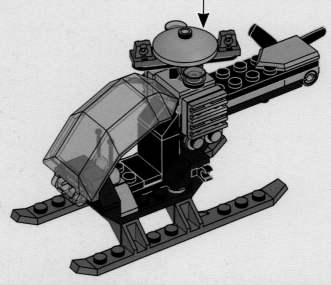

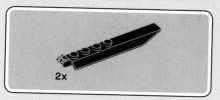

19

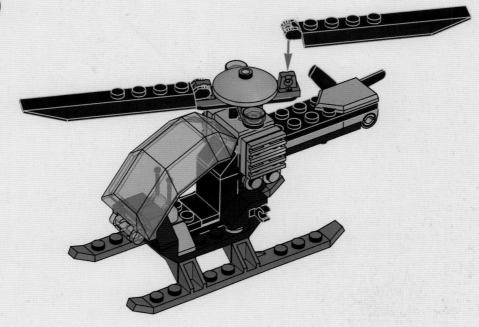

20

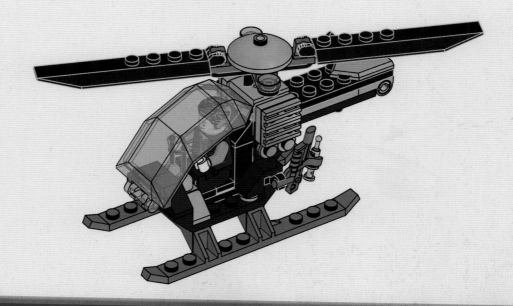

Senior Editors Selina Wood, Laura Palosuo
Project Art Editor Sam Bartlett
Senior Production Editor Jennifer Murray
Senior Production Controller Lloyd Robertson
Managing Editor Paula Regan
Managing Art Editor Jo Connor
Art Director Lisa Lanzarini
Publisher Julie Ferris
Publishing Director Mark Searle

Written by Julia March and Selina Wood
Inspirational models built by Rod Gillies
Photography by Gary Ombler

DK would like to thank Randi Sørensen, Heidi K. Jensen,
Paul Hansford, Martin Leighton Lindhardt, Marcos Bessa,
Luis Gómez Piedrahita Clausen, Brian Bering Larsen, and
Charlotte Neidhardt at the LEGO Group; Kurt Estes,
Susan Weber, Lauren Goldstein, and Megan Startz at
Universal Studios; and Jennette ElNaggar for proofreading.

First American Edition, 2020
Published in the United States by DK Publishing
1450 Broadway, Suite 801,
New York, New York 10018

Page design copyright © 2020 Dorling Kindersley Limited
DK, a Division of Penguin Random House LLC
20 21 22 23 24 10 9 8 7 6 5 4 3 2 1
001–316397–Aug/2020

LEGO, the LEGO logo, the Minifigure, and the
Brick and Knob configurations are trademarks
and/or copyrights of the LEGO Group.
©2020 The LEGO Group. All rights reserved.

Manufactured by Dorling Kindersley,
One Embassy Gardens, 8 Viaduct Gardens,
London SW11 7BW, under license from the LEGO Group.

© 2020 Jurassic World is a trademark
and copyright of Universal Studios
and Amblin Entertainment, Inc.
All rights reserved.

All rights reserved. Without limiting the rights under the
copyright reserved above, no part of this publication may be
reproduced, stored in or introduced into a retrieval system,
or transmitted, in any form, or by any means (electronic,
mechanical, photocopying, recording, or otherwise), without
the prior written permission of the copyright owner.
Published in Great Britain by Dorling Kindersley Limited.

A catalog record for this book is available
from the Library of Congress.
ISBN 978-1-4654-9327-9

DK books are available at special discounts when
purchased in bulk for sales promotions, premiums,
fund-raising, or educational use. For details, contact:
DK Publishing Special Markets, 1450 Broadway, Suite 801,
New York, New York 10018. SpecialSales@dk.com

Printed and bound in China

For the curious
www.dk.com
www.LEGO.com

TIME FOR
A WELL-EARNED
TREAT!